THE UP AND DOWN SPRING

ALSO BY JOHANNA HURWITZ

THE UP AND DOWN SPRING

Johanna Hurwitz

Interior illustrations by Gail Owens

AN
APPLE
PAPERBACK

SCHOLASTIC INC.
New York Toronto London Auckland Sydney

For all the children
up and down Spruce Place

ISBN 0-590-47736-6

12 11 10 9 8 7 6 5 4 3 2 1   4 5 6 7 8 9/9

Printed in the U.S.A.   40

First Scholastic printing, April 1994

Contents

1
Up in the Air

During February and into March, Rory Dunn and his best friend, Derek Curry, received many letters from Bolivia. However, none of this mail arrived with postage stamps from a South American country. Their letters were from a friend who lived in upstate New York. Her name was Bolivia Raab.

February 1

Dear Rory,

When is your spring break this year? My school closes April 10 and doesn't open again until April 20.

If you have the same vacation, wouldn't it be great if you could visit me in Ithaca? I've had so much fun my last two vacations in New Jersey. I know we'll have a great time here. I have a hundred plans already!

My mother is going to call your mother. My great-aunt and great-uncle, the Goldings, are planning a drive here this spring. My mother thought you could all come together.

I'm keeping my fingers crossed!

Your friend,

Bolivia

P.S. I'm sending the same letter to Derek.

Rory's letter had been waiting one day when he returned from school. As soon as he finished reading it, he raced over to Derek's house. Sure enough, there was Derek, reading his letter. Together the boys did a wild dance around Derek's house. Since both of Derek's parents were at work, no one complained about the noise. Then they went back over to Rory's house to show the invitations to Mrs. Dunn.

"It's very nice of Bolivia and her parents to invite you boys," said Rory's mother. "But I'll have to talk this over with your father and Derek's parents. We'll have to speak with the Goldings, too. It's quite a long drive for them to take with two passengers. Hasn't Bolivia flown when she's come here?"

Rory felt a chill go down his spine. The very thought of flying gave him the creeps.

"The Goldings won't mind taking us in the car," Rory said, trying to reassure his mother and himself.

"I want to go to Bolivia too," said Edna.

Edna was Rory's little sister. She was four years old but often seemed to think she was ten, almost eleven, like Rory and Derek.

"We'll see," said Mrs. Dunn, but Rory knew there was no way Edna would go with them to Ithaca.

Dear Bolivia,

Derek and I are counting the days until our trip.

The Goldings don't like to drive too many hours, so they are going to spend a night at a motel on the way to Ithaca and on the way back, too. Derek and I are going to share a room. We can stay up all night and watch TV and no one can stop us. Don't you wish you could be there? Ha! Ha! If you were, we wouldn't be going to see you.

Your friend,

Rory

February 10

Dear Bolivia,

Happy birthday! By the time I see you, I'll be eleven too. Derek will still be only ten until May 4.

I just heard your great-aunt had to go to the hospital. She got ~~newmonia~~ ~~neumonia~~

pneumonia. (I had to go check it in the dictionary because I knew I was spelling it wrong. But since it didn't even start with the letter n, I couldn't find it. So my mother had to tell me. Sometimes dictionaries are no use at all.)

Derek and I were really worried. But your great-uncle said she is coming home on Tuesday. Thank goodness. I bought her a get-well card when I bought you this one for your birthday.

Your friend,

Rory

February 28

Dear Rory,

Bad news. My great-aunt's doctor heard that we get tons of snow here in Ithaca—sometimes even in April—so he told her she should vacation in a warm place.

Do you think your parents and Derek's would let you travel here on your own? I always travel to Woodside by myself.

Maybe, maybe, maybe your parents will be able to arrange something.

Your hopeful friend,

Bolivia

March 14

Dear Rory,

You owe me a letter. So does Derek. Just because you're not coming is no reason not to write. I haven't given up hope.

Hey, I just thought of something. Maybe your parents and Derek's parents would buy you tickets to Ithaca as birthday presents.

Still your friend,

Bolivia

7

Dear Rory,

Happy birthday!

I already know what you got for a present! Your mother phoned my parents. So I know Derek is getting tickets as an early birthday present too. I actually already knew for a few days, but I promised to keep it a secret.

Don't be disappointed that you are taking a bus and not flying. There isn't even a major airport in Ithaca. We have a tiny one, but planes from Newark don't fly here. The reason I flew when I came to Woodside was that my parents were taking a plane for their trip from Buffalo. Also, my father makes so many business trips and has so many frequent-flyer miles that both times I visited you guys, I had free tickets.

Start packing! You'll be here in just over three weeks.

> Your friend who is
> counting the days,
>
> Bolivia

2
All Aboard

Even though they had been planning the trip for days and weeks, on the morning of departure there was a last-minute rush of activity at the Dunn household.

"Don't forget your old eyeglasses," Rory's mother called. "It's good to have a backup in case you break or lose your regular ones."

Rory had been wearing glasses since he was seven years old. In all this time he had never lost or broken a pair. So he thought his mother was a bit silly to worry about that. Still, he pulled everything out of his underwear drawer until he found his old glasses. They had been hidden under some socks. Rory tucked them into a corner of his suitcase.

"Here. I almost forgot this," said Mrs. Dunn,

breathlessly coming into Rory's room and handing him a gift-wrapped package.

"Is this for me?" asked Rory. He hadn't been expecting any presents this morning.

"Don't open it," said his mother, stopping him just in time. "It's a bread-and-butter gift for Bolivia's parents."

"Bread and butter?" Rory sniffed the package, which smelled strongly of perfume. It was the wrong shape for bread and butter, and besides, wouldn't butter melt?

"It's polite to give your host and hostess a gift when you stay at someone's home. It's just *called* a bread-and-butter present. It's really a box of soap."

Rory wondered if Bolivia's parents would like getting a box of soap. He knew *he* wouldn't. And even worse, the perfumed smell of the soap would get on everything in his suitcase. He'd smell like a flower garden or like a girl. When his mother wasn't looking, Rory took the package and put it into his backpack with his baseball cap, a book to read on the bus, his lunch, and a pack of chewing gum.

"Rory! Derek is here. We'd better leave now in case there is a lot of traffic."

Hearing his father's voice calling him, Rory quickly zipped up his suitcase. "Coming," he called.

Edna came running into his room. "I want to go," she cried. "I want to go to Bolivia."

"You're too little," said Rory.

"No I'm not!" cried Edna. She sat on top of Rory's suitcase. "I'm just the right size."

"I just mean you're too little to make such a big trip," said Rory.

Mrs. Dunn scooped up her daughter and gave her a hug. "Edna honey, if you and Rory both went away on a trip together, Daddy and I would be very lonely. Won't you stay and keep us company while Rory is gone?"

"Rory!" his father called again. "You don't want to miss your bus."

Rory grabbed his luggage and left his mother comforting Edna, who had begun howling with disappointment. Rory decided he wouldn't miss *her* at all. Mr. Dunn put his son's suitcase into the trunk while Rory said hello to Derek's parents. Derek was already sitting in the back of the car. Rory got into the front seat.

"What's that you've got?" Rory asked.

Derek was holding a shoe box tied with a piece of string. The lid of the box had holes punched in it.

"It's Hamlet," said Derek. Hamlet was Derek's hamster.

"Why did you have to bring him?" said Rory.

"My parents are going away too, you know," Derek replied. "There won't be anybody to take care of him. Besides, Hamlet and I have never been parted."

Derek had owned the hamster only since Christmas, three and a half months before. Rory turned back around in his seat. Derek worries too much, Rory thought.

Mr. Dunn beeped his car horn to signal good-bye, and the car took off. Mrs. Dunn and a still tearful Edna waved from the doorway of the house.

Fortunately there wasn't much traffic, and they arrived at the bus terminal on time. Almost before he knew it, Rory found himself boarding the bus with Derek. The bus started off exactly at 9:45. He was amazed at how many people had been waiting. Rory and Derek were lucky to get a double seat to themselves.

Rory's suitcase was in the luggage compartment in the side of the bus. He had put his backpack on the overhead rack. He stood and pulled down the pack to take out his book, but as he unzipped it, he got a whiff of a strong, sweet scent. It was that present his mother had given him for Bolivia's parents. Now his lunch was going to smell and taste like soap and flowers. Rory took the gift out of the pack and pushed it to the back of the rack. He'd leave it there until they reached Ithaca.

"Too bad we're not flying," said Derek when Rory sat down again. "That would have been super perfect."

"Yeah," said Rory, pretending to agree. He was glad that during all the planning for this trip, no one had guessed he was afraid of flying. The day Rory's mother had phoned the airlines to check ticket prices, Rory was just about to say he had changed his mind and didn't want to make the trip. Thank goodness his mother began investigating bus schedules. It had been a close shave. Even though they were best friends, Rory didn't want Derek to know. He was afraid either he'd laugh his head off or he'd think Rory was nuts. There probably wasn't another eleven-year-old boy in the whole world who wouldn't give anything for the chance to fly.

"We've never flown anywhere," Derek complained. "This trip is going to take five and a half hours. If we flew, we'd be there in an hour."

"You can see more on a bus," Rory pointed out to Derek, who had the window seat. "What can you see in an airplane? Just clouds."

Somewhere Rory had read that two of his favorite science-fiction writers, Isaac Asimov and Ray Bradbury, never took airplanes. What did they know about air travel that he and Derek and maybe even the pilot didn't know?

Derek shifted in his seat and put the shoe box with Hamlet on the floor by his feet.

"Let's take him out," said Rory.

"No," said Derek. "I don't want to open the box until we get to Bolivia's."

Both boys opened their books. But it was hard to concentrate. After a while the motion of the bus made Rory feel sleepy. He hadn't slept much the night before, thinking about the trip. He dozed off now and woke with a start when the bus stopped. Several new passengers were getting on. They

14

looked like college students. In fact, most of the passengers on the bus looked like college students. The bus would be stopping in several college towns before it reached Ithaca.

There was a meal stop scheduled at 1:20 in the afternoon, when the bus would wait at a diner in Binghamton, New York. But the boy's mothers knew they would be hungry long before that. By 11:30 Rory and Derek had finished their sandwiches, apples, and cookies. Rory had a tangerine, which he was going to save till later. They were to arrive in Ithaca at 3:10 P.M., an awfully long way off.

"I'm going to the bathroom," said Derek. There was actually a little toilet and sink in a tiny closet-size room in the rear of the bus. "You can have a turn at the window seat now," he offered Rory.

"Thanks," said Rory. But he was already bored with craning his head to look out the window at trees that hadn't yet begun to grow leaves and houses that all looked pretty much the same. Occasionally they passed a field with a few horses or a pond. None of it was terribly exciting.

He wondered how Hamlet was doing, cooped up in the dark little box on the floor. He was proba-

15

bly as bored as they were. Rory reached down and picked up the box. He tried peeking through the little air holes, but they were too small and it was too dark inside to see anything. Carefully he untied the knot in the string and opened the box. He stroked the soft fur on the hamster. Then he put the box on Derek's seat and took Hamlet out.

"How do you like traveling?" he whispered.

As if in response to the question, the hamster shot out of Rory's hand and landed with a soft *thud* on the floor. Before Rory had a chance to lean down and grab him, the hamster scampered down the aisle toward the front of the bus.

Rory jumped up to follow.

"Hamlet. Hamlet," he called after the tiny runaway creature.

He got down on his hands and knees, but he saw only feet, a gum wrapper, and a broken pen on the grimy floor of the bus.

"Hamlet. Hamlet. Where are you?" he called a little louder.

"You're reciting your lines wrong, kid," a college student said. "It goes 'O Romeo, Romeo, wherefore art thou Romeo?' You've got your Shakespearean plays mixed up."

16

"No, no. I'm not reciting anything," said Rory. "I'm looking for Hamlet, my friend's hamster. He got out of his box."

"I'll help you," said the student.

Now there were two people crawling around on the floor.

"What's going on down there?" asked a woman as Rory crawled past her seat.

"We're looking for a hamster," Rory explained.

Soon everyone on the bus was looking for Hamlet. Derek, who had returned to his seat and found an empty box on it, was calling out instructions.

The bus slowed for one of its stops. "Don't open the door," shouted Derek. "He might get off."

"Is this his stop?" asked the driver.

"No, no," said Rory. "He's going to Ithaca."

Just at that moment Hamlet was discovered. He had made it all the way to the front of the bus. A girl with a Binghamton sweatshirt stood up, cupping the hamster in her hands.

"I found him. Do I get a prize?" she asked.

"I have a tangerine left from my lunch," said Rory. "Would you like that?" He was very relieved that the hamster had been found.

"Great!" said the girl. "I'm starving."

Derek took his hamster and put him back in the box, Rory got the tangerine and gave it to the girl, and the bus driver opened and shut the door of the bus, even though no one got off and no one got on.

The search for the hamster had gotten many of the passengers in a festive mood. People who had been dozing were talking and laughing now. One man told his seatmate that he used to have a guinea pig when he was young. And someone else wanted to get a kitten, but it wasn't allowed in his college dorm.

Rory sat down next to Derek. He looked at his watch. "Only three and a half hours to go," he said. Then he quickly closed his eyes and pretended to be sleeping. Thank goodness Hamlet had been all right. He knew Derek must have guessed how the hamster had gotten out of his box. As always, Rory had done it. Rory vowed silently that he wouldn't do anything stupid like that again. He didn't want anything to spoil their vacation. He knew Derek felt that way too.

3
Bolivia's Big Plan

"Suppose no one is here to meet us?" Derek asked in a worried voice. His wristwatch showed that it was 3:00 P.M., and they were nearing their destination.

"They'll be here," said Rory as he pulled his backpack down from the overhead rack.

"Are you nervous?" asked Derek.

"About what?"

"Visiting strange people and staying in their home and all."

"Bolivia's not strange," Rory said. "She's unusual, that's for sure; but she's not strange."

"I don't mean Bolivia. I mean we don't even know her parents, and we're going to be sleeping in their house for six nights."

21

"You went to summer camp last year and you didn't know anyone there," Rory pointed out.

"I guess you're right," said Derek.

"Don't worry. We're going to have a great time," Rory said as the bus slowed to a halt.

Many people were getting off here. This was the stop for Cornell University and Ithaca College. Quite a few of the passengers were probably students at these schools.

"Look at that!" someone ahead of Rory and Derek shouted.

Rory looked up and saw a large banner and a pair of helium balloons. The banner read, WELCOME, FRIENDS OF BOLIVIA.

"Is anyone on this bus the ambassador from Bolivia?" someone asked.

Rory and Derek began laughing as they raced toward the banner. Of course it had nothing to do with South America or politics. Sure enough, there was Bolivia, and at either end of the poles holding up the banner stood one of her parents. Her father had hair almost as red as Bolivia's, and a red beard as well. Her mother had a big grin that matched her daughter's.

"What a neat sign!" said Derek.

"I couldn't decide what to say," said Bolivia. "If I'd written 'Welcome, Rory and Derek,' Derek might have been insulted that his name wasn't first. And if I'd put Derek's name first, Rory might not have liked it."

"How was the ride?" Bolivia's mother asked the boys.

"Hamlet got lost, but we found him," said Derek.

And so, as if resuming a conversation left unfinished the last time they were together, the three friends followed Mr. and Mrs. Raab and the banner and the balloons into the parking area. It wasn't easy to get the balloons into the car with all the luggage and Hamlet's shoe box.

"I can't drive if those balloons block the back window," Mr. Raab said.

"No problem," said Bolivia. She yanked the strings and pulled the balloons out of the car. Then she left her parents and Rory and Derek in the car as she presented the balloons to a mother pushing a stroller with two small children in it. It was a good idea, Rory had to admit. Bolivia was always full of good ideas. That's why they liked her so much.

As soon as they reached Bolivia's house, the boys

23

wanted to see her pet parrot, Lucette. She took them into a glassed-in sun porch that was filled with plants. "My father has a green thumb," said Bolivia. "I can tell you the Latin name of every one of these."

"Show us what you've taught Lucette," said Rory.

The parrot sat on a perch in the center of the room. Her cage was littered with shells from sunflower seeds and half an apple with several bites missing.

"Who is here?" Bolivia asked the bird.

The parrot stopped preening her bright green feathers and blinked her black eyes. She looked wise and knowing, as if she recognized the boys. Then she squawked loudly, "Not today. Come again."

"Who is here?" Bolivia repeated.

This time there was no reaction at all from Lucette.

"Who is here?" Bolivia asked for a third time.

"Roryderek. Roryderek."

"She said it! She said our names!" shouted Rory.

"I've been working on it for weeks," said Bolivia proudly. "But I haven't been able to get her to reverse the names. I thought it would be fair if half the time she said 'Derekrory.' But somehow she's never mastered that one."

"I don't mind," said Derek. Hamlet couldn't say anything. "Wait, that reminds me," he said. "What did I do with Hamlet?"

"You put the box down with your luggage," Bolivia said. "Come on. I'll show you guys where you're going to sleep."

They went back to the living room, and the boys retrieved their suitcases.

"Do you have a bigger box that Hamlet can stay in while we're here?" asked Derek.

"We have everything," Bolivia assured him. "Look. This is the room you'll be in." She showed the boys a room with bookshelves on two walls. There was a chest of drawers, and against the far wall there was a couch and a window. "This opens up into a double bed," Bolivia explained, patting the couch. "The bathroom is right across the hall."

Derek put his bag down on the couch and unfastened it. He pulled out a flat, gift-wrapped package. "This is a present for your parents," he said. "My mother sent it. She said it's a bread-and-butter gift."

"I've got one too," said Rory. He unzipped his backpack to get the present. Suddenly his face turned red as he remembered. "I left the package on the bus." The bus driver wouldn't know who the gift on the overhead rack belonged to. Rory wondered if he would use the perfumed soap to take a shower that night.

"This is an art book," said Derek. "I hope your parents don't already have it. They sure have a lot of books."

Seeing Derek with a gift, Rory felt very uncomfortable about not having anything for Bolivia's parents. But then he remembered that his father had given him some money to take with him. He would find a way to buy something for the Raabs as soon as he could. It would be something better than smelly, perfumed soap, too.

After seeing that Hamlet was happy inside his shoe box, Rory and Derek and Bolivia toured the rest of the house. Bolivia showed them her room, and the big room that her parents shared as an office. There were two computers, and bookshelves on all four walls. The Raabs sure seemed to own a lot of books, Rory thought. Even more than his father had at home, and he was an English teacher.

Bolivia's parents were archeologists. They had bookshelves everywhere, even in the kitchen.

"I collect old cookbooks," Mrs. Raab told Rory. "Sometimes on archeological digs we've found old cooking utensils. And we've even discovered clay jars filled with rice or grain from thousands of years ago."

"Can you still eat it?" asked Derek. There was a peculiar aroma in the kitchen. He imagined sitting down to a dinner of dinosaur stew and rice.

"You probably *could* eat it, but we save it to exhibit in the museum," said Mrs. Raab.

The kitchen light flickered overhead. "Oh, that light," Mrs. Raab complained. "Why does it always do that?"

"Wait till you see what we're having for supper," said Bolivia as they all sat down to eat. "It was my idea."

"What's in it?" asked Derek. He and Rory looked suspiciously at the large, steaming casserole that Mrs. Raab brought to the table. The food was a strange yellow color. And it wasn't something that either Mrs. Dunn or Mrs. Curry had ever made for supper.

"Can't you guess?" asked Bolivia, grinning.

27

Rory and Derek shook their heads.

"Curry! Haven't you ever had it?" Bolivia asked. "It's your *name,* after all. Derek Curry should eat curry at least once. I would, if that was my name."

"What is curry?" asked Derek.

"Curry's a spice used in Indian dishes. This is chicken curry that we're having tonight. Don't worry, you'll love it."

"Maybe," said Derek doubtfully.

"My name isn't curry," said Rory. "I don't see why I should have to eat it."

"That's true," said Bolivia. "But you see, it's already done. Get it: Dunn-done?" She laughed at her own joke.

"We like puns and wordplays around here," said Mr. Raab, smiling.

The boys looked at each other unhappily.

"Too bad your last name isn't McDonald," said Rory.

Derek nodded in agreement.

"Listen, fellows," said Mrs. Raab. "It was Bolivia's idea to have curry for supper tonight. And when she gets an idea, it's difficult to change her mind. But curry has an unusual taste, and if you don't like it, you don't have to eat it. I can make you each a hamburger."

The boys were relieved by this offer. But of course, they still had to try the curry, just to be polite. The good news was that the chicken curry with rice, from this century and not from prehistoric times, tasted much better than it looked or smelled. It probably helped, Rory thought, that he hadn't eaten anything since his early lunch on the bus. That, plus a piece of pie and a glass of milk at the diner, was all he'd eaten that day. He had been too excited to eat any breakfast. So Mrs. Raab didn't make any hamburgers, and Rory even had second helpings of the chicken curry.

"I guess you *done* a good thing when you suggested this for dinner," he told Bolivia.

"Rory Dunn, I can see you're ready to become a member of our pun club," said Bolivia's father.

That made Rory feel pretty good.

Then Mrs. Raab said, "Bolivia, have you told the boys the big plan?"

"What big plan?" asked Rory and Derek together.

"Well, since the tickets to come here were your

birthday presents," said Bolivia, "I thought we should do something special to celebrate your birthdays—and mine, too, even though I live here and I've already had my birthday."

"Great," said Rory.

"I wanted to buy you a present, but I didn't have enough money saved. Besides, I figured I should get something too, since we're all celebrating our birthdays. Then Uncle Harold came to my rescue. He offered me something for my birthday that's better than money."

"What's better than money?" asked Rory.

"You'll see."

"You mean you aren't going to tell us?" said Rory. "No fair."

"Then it wouldn't be a surprise."

"I don't care," said Rory.

"Me neither," said Derek.

"Go ahead. Tell them," urged Bolivia's father.

Bolivia's grin was even bigger than usual. "My uncle Harold has a pilot's license. And he says that he'll take all three of us up together in one of those little propeller planes. They don't fly as high as a jet, but you get a super aerial view of everything."

"Wow," said Derek. "That's fantastic. Just this

morning I told Rory I wished we could have flown here. And now we're going to have a chance."

Rory wished he hadn't taken that second helping of the curry. His stomach wasn't taking Bolivia's news very well.

"When are we going?" asked Derek.

"The day after tomorrow, if the weather is good," said Bolivia.

Rory felt a glimmer of hope. Maybe, just maybe, if he was lucky, there would be a storm the day after tomorrow. Maybe there would be a small tornado, even. Rory put his hands in his lap, where no one could see them. He crossed his fingers on both hands. A little hurricane or an earthquake would be okay too, he thought.

4
A Long Night in a Strange Bed

After supper Mrs. Raab reminded the boys to phone their parents. "I want them to know that you arrived here safely," she said.

Rory called home first. It seemed strange to be so many miles away from the home he had been in that morning. "How are you?" he asked his mother.

"Your father and I are just fine," Mrs. Dunn replied. "But Edna seems to be coming down with something. I think she has a slight fever."

"She's probably just mad because she didn't get to go with us," said Rory.

"Maybe," said Mrs. Dunn. "How are you? Are you having a good time?"

"Oh, great," said Rory without much enthusiasm. He was trying hard not to think about Bolivia's big plan.

Then Derek phoned his parents. They were leaving the next day for a cruise, so he wouldn't be able to call them again. When Mrs. Raab took the phone from Derek to thank his mother for the gift, Rory winced. He thought again about the box of soap that he had left on the bus. Everything about this visit seemed to be going wrong.

The first thing tomorrow, Rory decided, he would go out and buy a gift for the Raabs. He wished he could do something about the plane ride and Bolivia's uncle as easily.

When the phone calls were completed, Bolivia took the boys to see her room. Because she had traveled so much with her parents, she had all sorts of souvenirs from all sorts of places.

There was a bank that looked like a wooden shoe. It had come from Holland. She had a miniature Eiffel Tower from France, and a clock that looked like Big Ben. That was a famous clock in London, Bolivia explained. She had a set of carved wooden camels that her parents had bought her in Israel, and a funny hat of bright red cloth with a black tassel that her parents had brought back from

Turkey. "Sometimes its called a tarboosh, but most people here call it a fez," said Bolivia.

Rory was sure he had seen people wearing them in the movies. "Can I try it on?" he asked.

So first he and then Derek tried on the Turkish hat. Then Derek remembered that he had brought his camera with him. He went and got it from his suitcase, so Bolivia could take a picture of him wearing the fez. Then he photographed Rory and Bolivia modeling the hat too.

"Too bad there's only one. It would be fun to have a picture of all three of us wearing this hat," said Rory, touching the deep red felt of the fez.

The three kids went back into the living room. Derek took a photograph of Bolivia's parents.

Bolivia looked at her wristwatch. "Time for games," she announced.

"What games?" asked Rory.

"Bolivia made a schedule," said Mr. Raab. "She has planned every minute of your visit."

"I don't want us to waste any time," said Bolivia. "Eight to nine-thirty is time for games." She pulled out a backgammon set from a pile on the table. "We can take turns."

Derek caught Rory's eye. Bolivia had more ideas

than anyone they knew. But she could also be very bossy sometimes.

"We don't have to *do* something every second," said Rory. "Sometimes it's fun not to do anything at all. We could just sit around and watch TV."

"I guess you didn't notice," said Bolivia. "We don't have a television set."

"You don't have a television?" gasped Rory. He had never heard of such a thing.

"Can't your parents afford it?" asked Derek.

"Of course we can afford a TV," said Bolivia. "We don't want one. We prefer to spend our time in other ways. And now we're going to play backgammon."

"What is backgammon?" asked Derek.

"It's a game," Bolivia said. "You'll love it." So for the next hour and a half, Bolivia taught the boys to play backgammon. At first Rory felt very grumpy. If he'd known that he was going to be spending his whole vacation without television, Rory thought, he might not have wanted to come. But after a while he got caught up in the game, and in the end he and Derek, playing as a team, managed to beat Bolivia twice.

"It just means that I'm a great teacher," said Bolivia.

When it was bedtime, Bolivia showed the boys how to open the couch. "I wish we could stay awake every minute," Bolivia said. "You guys are only going to be here for six days, and we're going to waste half of it sleeping."

"Yeah," Derek agreed. But even as he said it, a yawn escaped him.

It took a while to prepare for bed. The boys took turns in the bathroom, and Derek checked on Hamlet. The hamster had been moved to a larger box, and Bolivia's father had even found some window screening to put on top of it, so there was plenty of air and it was easy to peek in.

Before the boys went to sleep, Derek remembered that he had brought in his suitcase a little alarm clock from home. He set it for 7:00 A.M. and wound it up. "If we get up early, we'll have more time to do things," he said, putting the clock on the chest across the room.

Mr. Raab came in to check that the boys were settled comfortably. "Good night, fellows," he said as he turned off the light for them.

37

"He's nice, isn't he?" Derek whispered in the dark.

"Yeah," Rory answered. "Bolivia's mother is nice too. Even if they are a little weird. Imagine not wanting to own a TV."

"Everybody is different, I guess," said Derek, yawning.

"What do you think of Bolivia's surprise?" Rory asked carefully. Maybe Derek was having second thoughts about going up in a small airplane.

"I can't wait," said Derek.

"Me too," said Rory, trying to make his voice sound like he was excited.

Derek yawned again.

The sofa was comfortable, Rory thought, but still, it wasn't his own bed at home. The window was in the wrong place too. He guessed no bed could ever be as comfortable as your own bed.

"I hope Hamlet is all right," said Derek.

Rory couldn't imagine that the pile of cut-up newspaper in Ithaca was much different for Hamlet than the cut-up newspaper in his cage in Woodside, New Jersey.

Rory listened in the dark. He couldn't hear the hamster. Probably he was fast asleep. The only sounds Rory could hear were Derek's breathing and the *tick-tock* of the alarm clock.

"Your clock sure makes a lot of noise," he said to Derek.

Derek didn't answer.

"The alarm clock I have at home doesn't make any noise," said Rory.

Again there was no answer from Derek. Rory gave his friend a little poke. "Are you asleep?" he asked.

No answer came, except the steady breathing that showed Derek was indeed asleep.

Rory turned over on his side. He lay in the dark and thought about the airplane ride he was supposed to take with Bolivia and Derek. He wished the visit to Bolivia was over already and he was safely back home in his own bed. But wishing wasn't the answer. He had to think of a plan to avoid going up if the weather let him down. Maybe he could say he had a stomach ache or a sore throat or some other temporary ailment that would keep him on the ground. That way Bolivia and Derek could have their flight and he could stay safely here at the house.

He turned over again. He wished he could fall

asleep so he wouldn't have to think about it. But that darn clock was making so much noise, it was impossible. Quietly, so as not to awaken Derek, Rory got out of bed. In the dark he felt his way toward the chest. He banged his knee on a chair, but the sound didn't wake Derek. Rory felt for the clock in the dark. It wasn't an electric clock, so he couldn't stop the ticking by unplugging it. He would have to muffle the sound. He opened the top drawer of the chest and put the clock inside, under Derek's clothes. When the drawer was closed, you could hardly hear the ticking at all.

Rory got back into bed and pulled the covers up over himself. Maybe now he could finally fall asleep.

Sometime in the middle of the night, Rory realized that he had been asleep. Once again he heard the clock ticking noisily. How had the sound become so loud through the drawer? When he couldn't fall back asleep, he got out of bed and cautiously approached the chest of drawers. Somehow the clock had returned to the top of the chest.

Rory put the clock inside the drawer again and closed it. It took longer to fall asleep the second time, but eventually he did. And he didn't wake until seven o'clock in the morning, when the alarm woke him up.

Derek jumped out of bed and shut it off. "Something funny is going on," he said. "Twice I woke up during the night and the clock I put on top of the chest was inside one of the drawers."

"Something funny *is* going on," said Rory. "It was keeping me awake, so I put it in the drawer, and it kept getting back out again."

"I did that. I'd wake up when I couldn't hear the ticking."

"It looks like we took turns all night," said Rory.

"No wonder I still feel sleepy," said Derek.

"We could go back to sleep for another ten minutes," Rory suggested.

"Good idea."

So with the alarm turned off and the clock ticking away on top of the chest of drawers, both Rory and Derek went back to bed for another ten minutes.

Bolivia woke them two hours later.

"Hey, you guys. Wake up already!" she said, knocking on their door. "It's time for breakfast. It's almost time for lunch, for goodness' sake."

It was time for the second day of their visit.

5
The
Bread-and-Butter
Gift

While the boys ate French toast, Bolivia told them the plans for the day. She seemed to have made arrangements for every minute of the vacation.

"This morning I'm going to show you around town. I want you to see where my school is and the park, places like that. We come back here for lunch, and then this afternoon we go swimming at the college. You remembered to bring your bathing suits, didn't you?"

"Sure," said Derek.

"Good," Bolivia continued, consulting her schedule. "Then this evening we have tickets to a show at the college theater."

42

"What are we going to see?" asked Rory. He had been to a couple of shows at the community playhouse in Woodside. And last year the school district had put on *Guys and Dolls,* and his father had had a big part in it.

"Wait and see," said Bolivia, grinning at Rory. "I want to surprise you.".

Rory tried to catch Derek's eye, but Derek was calmly helping himself to another slice of Mrs. Raab's French toast. Clearly he had decided to take Bolivia's plans in stride.

"You two sure eat a lot," Bolivia said impatiently as Rory, too, reached for a second helping. "We'll never get going if you guys don't stop eating breakfast."

"Hey, take it easy. Where's the fire? This is our vacation," Rory said. "We shouldn't have to rush."

Finally breakfast was over. The boys put on their jackets and followed Bolivia. Rory checked that he had his wallet with his money. He wanted to buy postcards to mail home, and he wanted to buy a gift for the Raabs, too, even if shopping wasn't one of Bolivia's plans.

It was a bright, crisp spring day. There was no

hint of a brewing storm, Rory noted regretfully to himself as the trio set out walking along State Street.

"I hope the weather stays just like this tomorrow," said Bolivia.

"Couldn't he take us another day?" asked Derek.

"Not this week. He can take me up another time, but you guys won't be here. I think we should just have a positive attitude. Think sun!"

Rory closed his eyes and pretended he was thinking about sun. But actually he was thinking about rain. He opened his eyes and looked at Bolivia. She was pretty smart, but she didn't know how to read minds. At least, he didn't think she did.

They crossed a street and walked a few more blocks.

"Here's my school," said Bolivia as they approached a red-brick building. "I wish it was open so I could show you my classroom."

"If it was open, you'd have to be inside. You wouldn't be on vacation, and we wouldn't have come to visit," Rory pointed out.

"True," Bolivia agreed. "But I wanted you to see the diorama I made for social studies. It's an Egyptian tomb with a mummy. I made it out of chicken bones wrapped in bits of an old sheet."

The boys stared at Bolivia in admiration. They had studied ancient Egypt too, but neither of them had done anything that interesting or that weird.

"Where can we get postcards?" Rory asked. "I promised my parents I'd send one. And I want to send one to Edna, too."

"There's a stationery shop on the next block," said Bolivia, leading the way.

In the stationery shop Rory picked out a pair of postcards, and Derek also bought two. "I'm sending one to my parents even if they aren't going to be home," he explained. He also bought a card to send to his grandparents.

The stationery store didn't sell stamps, so they walked toward the post office.

"I want to get a present for your parents," Rory told Bolivia.

"Oh, you don't have to do that," Bolivia said.

"You're supposed to bring a bread-and-butter gift when you stay at someone's home. Derek did. My mother gave me one too, but I left it on the bus by mistake."

45

"How about buying some real bread and but-ter?" Bolivia suggested.

"Bread and butter for a bread-and-butter gift? I really like that," said Rory.

"I'll tell you where to go while Derek and I go on to the post office for stamps," said Bolivia. "We'll save time that way."

"No problem," said Rory.

Bolivia explained to Rory how to find the bak-ery. "Then you just walk four blocks back to State Street. You remember the number of my house?" she asked him.

"Sixty-eight?"

"Close, but not close enough," said Bolivia. "It's *eight* six eight. Don't forget. Three numbers, Eight Six Eight East State Street."

"Got it," said Rory. "I won't forget."

Rory set off to the bakery. He smelled it a block away—the most wonderful scent of cinnamon and chocolate and freshly baked bread. There was a dish of broken cookies on the counter, and Rory sampled a couple of pieces while he waited his turn.

The cookies were delicious, but since this was a bread-and-butter gift, he asked for a large loaf of the cinnamon bread. "Do you sell butter?" he asked.

"We have milk over in that case, but no butter," said the saleswoman. Seeing the disappointed look on Rory's face, she added, "You could get butter at the supermarket. It's just two blocks from here."

"Thanks," said Rory. It would just take him a few extra minutes to pick up the butter. He paid for the bread and asked the saleswoman for directions to the supermarket.

The two blocks turned out to be very long ones, but at last Rory reached the supermarket. The dairy case wasn't near the meat counter, the way it was back home. There was sweet butter and salt butter. Sweet butter sounded better for cinnamon bread, so Rory picked out a half-pound package and stood in line. There wasn't an express line, and Rory found himself behind several wagons piled high with groceries.

After he had been standing in line for ages, the woman ahead of him turned around and noticed him.

"Is that all you have?" she said. "Here, go ahead of me."

That gave Rory the idea of asking each person in line if he could move ahead. Three of them agreed. The fourth was having her groceries rung up, so Rory couldn't get ahead of her. She had more groceries than all the other people in the line put together. In fact, it took two wagons to hold all of her purchases. Rory wondered how large her family was. Maybe she went shopping only once a month or once every two months. It was just his luck that he was standing behind her on the day she ran out of food at home.

Finally Rory was able to pay for the half pound of butter. He clutched the two bags and started back to Bolivia's house. A wind had begun blowing since he had gone into the bakery. The sun was still shining, but it seemed much colder than it had been before. Maybe it was a sign that the weather was changing.

Rory closed the top button on his jacket and wished that he had worn his cap. He tried to find the bakery again. He would know how to go on from there. Rory walked for three blocks before he realized that he must be going in the wrong direction. He was passing a small park he didn't remember passing before.

He turned around and started back in the opposite direction. This time he went four blocks, but there was no sign of the bakery. He stood trying to figure out where he was, but as he had never been here before, it didn't really mean much that he was at Cascadilla Street.

"I'm looking for a bakery," Rory told a man who was walking his dog.

"I buy everything at the supermarket," the man said.

Luckily Rory remembered that he was holding the bag with the cinnamon bread. The name of the bakery and its address were printed right on the bag!

"Albany Street is in that direction," said the man.

"Thanks," said Rory, and he set off.

He realized that by now Bolivia and Derek must be back home. He hoped they weren't worrying about him. He felt pretty stupid about getting lost. He would tell them that there was a long line in the bakery. They didn't have to know that he had walked in the wrong direction. He put the bag with the butter into the larger bag with the bread and put his free hand into his pocket to keep it warm.

Sniffing the air, he began to smell the cinnamon-and-chocolate odor once again. Only this time it smelled twice as good as it had before, because now it meant he was walking in the right direction.

He kept going another block, and there was the bakery. Now all he had to do was find State Street and the number of Bolivia's house. There were three numbers, he reminded himself. Six eight six.

Rory asked a boy who was about his age, "Which way is State Street?"

"I don't know."

"Don't you live around here?" asked Rory.

"I don't think it's near my house," said the boy. "I live on North Cayuga."

Rory looked around for someone else he could ask. A woman came out of the bakery.

"Which way to State Street?" he asked.

"East or West?" asked the woman.

Uh-oh, thought Rory. He didn't remember. "I don't think it matters," he said, hoping he was right. "As long as I find State Street, I think I can find my way."

The woman told Rory to turn left and go two blocks. "Cross Seneca Street, and the next street you come to is State."

"I hope I don't run into Bolivia," Rory said, half to himself.

"Bolivia?" said the woman, laughing. "You're on the wrong continent."

Rory didn't feel like explaining that this Bolivia was a girl and he didn't want her to know he was lost. He thanked the woman for the directions and started off. "Six eight six," he chanted. "Six eight six."

He shifted the bag with the bread and butter from one hand to the other so he could give the first one a rest and a chance to warm up inside his pocket.

He found State Street without any problem and began walking from number seven hundred down. It seemed awfully far to go. He hoped he had the address right. He wished he had written more letters to Bolivia during the fall and winter. Then he would have been more sure of her address. Seven ninety-two, seven ninety, seven eighty-eight. Rory began to feel hungry. He was tempted to take a slice of the bread from the bag, but he resisted. Seven seventy-four. Seven seventy-two.

Rory waited for a traffic light. He opened the bag of bread and sniffed inside. He was starving.

Would Mrs. Raab notice if he took one little slice? Probably not. He opened the plastic wrap and took a slice from the center of the loaf. It was the best thing he had ever eaten in his life. He had certainly bought a terrific gift for Mrs. Raab.

The first slice of bread was so good that Rory couldn't resist taking a second one. Who would care that two slices were missing from a whole loaf of bread?

Rory was nearing six eight six and his sixth slice of cinnamon bread when a car pulled up alongside him.

"Rory!" a voice called out to him. It was Bolivia. "What are you doing here?"

"I'm going to your house, of course," said Rory, surprised to see Derek and Bolivia and Mrs. Raab all looking at him from the car.

"You're going in the wrong direction," Bolivia said.

"Six eight six?" said Rory.

"Eight six eight," said Bolivia. "We thought you were lost, and you were."

"I would have found you eventually," said Rory as he climbed into the car next to Derek. It felt

great to sit down after his long walk, and it was warm inside the car too.

"Weren't you scared?" asked Derek.

"Gosh, no. Just cold and hungry. I knew I'd find Bolivia's house eventually. I just didn't want everyone to be worried about me," Rory said.

"I would have been scared," said Derek. "Walking around in a strange town when you don't even know anyone."

Rory looked at Derek in surprise. It just hadn't occurred to him to be frightened.

"You really messed up the schedule," said Bolivia.

"Sorry," said Rory, without feeling sorry in the least.

Mrs. Raab made a U-turn and started back in the direction that Rory had just come from.

"Mrs. Raab," said Rory. "Could I ask you a favor?"

"Anything within reason."

"Could we stop at that bakery on Albany Street? I bought you a loaf of bread as a bread-and-butter gift, but I got so hungry that I ate most of it."

"No problem," said Mrs. Raab.

54

"Give us some too," said Bolivia. "We've all missed lunch looking for you.

So the remainder of the first loaf of cinammon bread was eaten before they even reached the bakery. But the second loaf that Rory bought was given to Mrs. Raab untouched. In fact, to be on the safe side, Rory had told the saleswoman to leave the loaf unsliced.

6
More Plans

"It's too late to go swimming," complained Bolivia when the three friends finally sat down to eat a late meal.

"It's not the end of the world if we don't go today," said Rory, biting into his sandwich. "We can go tomorrow, instead."

"We can't go tomorrow. Tomorrow we're going up in the plane with my uncle. And the next day I've arranged—"

"Bolivia," Mrs. Raab interrupted. "Perhaps Rory and Derek don't want you to plan every minute for them."

"I don't mind. Especially about the airplane ride," said Derek.

"See," said Bolivia. "That was *my* idea. And if

Rory hadn't gotten lost, we would have had a great time swimming this afternoon too."

"I wasn't lost," said Rory. "I just didn't know I was going in the wrong direction. I would have figured it out before long. You didn't give me a chance."

"We couldn't wait all day until you turned up again. You were lost," said Bolivia.

"You were," Derek agreed.

As they spoke, the kitchen light flickered again.

"I'll have to take care of that one of these days," Mrs. Raab said. "Since you kids didn't go swimming, you have time to read the story of the ballet you are going to see this evening."

"Ballet?" gasped Rory. "You didn't tell us we were going to the ballet." He would have said something more if Bolivia's mother hadn't been sitting across the table from him.

"It was my surprise," said Bolivia.

Rory didn't say another word. He waited until they had left the kitchen and were in Bolivia's room.

"I thought we were going to a show," he exploded. "Not some sissy ballet."

"A ballet is a type of show," said Bolivia. "The

Ithaca Ballet Company is first-rate. And it's not sissy stuff at all. Have you ever seen the muscles on the dancers? I bet you haven't ever even seen a ballet."

"I have so seen ballet," said Rory. "On television. And it stinks." He turned to Derek to back him up.

"Maybe it won't be so bad," said Derek.

"Don't you remember when my mother was watching ballet on TV and we were laughing the whole time?" Rory jumped up from the floor where he was sitting and pretended to be a dancer. He kicked his foot up into the air, just missing Derek's head.

"Hey, watch it," Derek protested. "This is the only head I've got."

"When you are a guest at someone's home, you should be more agreeable," Bolivia told Rory.

"Oh, yeah? Well, when someone is a guest in your house, you ought to think about what *they* like and what *they* don't like. You shouldn't make a hundred plans for them without asking them what they want to do."

"Listen," said Derek, trying to make peace between them. "Tonight we go to the ballet. Tomorrow we're going up in the airplane. We can *all* enjoy that."

Rory sat down hard on Bolivia's bed and didn't say a word. Things were getting worse and worse. Now his best friend Derek was saying he should sit through the ballet because the next day they would be rewarded with the airplane flight. Why hadn't he just stayed home in Woodside? Rory wondered. At home, at least he could have watched television. After all, a vacation was for taking it easy.

"Come on, Rory," said Derek. "It won't be terrible."

"Yes, it will," said Rory. He wasn't going to forgive Bolivia so quickly. He wanted her to know that sitting through the ballet tonight would be a real sacrifice on his part.

"Your life is going to be awfully boring if you don't try new things," Bolivia said. "I'm always trying new things. I went to the home games of the Cornell football team last fall. I go to all the new shows at the Johnson Museum of Art. And I want my father to take us to the Corning Glass Museum. You can see how glass is made there."

"I wish we had been here for the football games," said Rory. He wished he'd known that his visit to Bolivia was going to be like one school cultural trip after another.

"Maybe next time you can visit during the fall, when the team is playing."

"Yeah," said Rory. It seemed unlikely to him that he would ever come back for a second visit. This one wasn't going the way he had hoped at all.

"What time do we go to this ballet?" asked Derek, relieved that Rory had finished arguing about the evening's plans.

"Not till after supper," said Bolivia. "We have time to play a game now. You can pick, Rory. Anything you want," she offered.

"Let's play a killer game of Monopoly," said Rory. "I bet I can wipe you out in no time."

"Oh, yeah? That's what you think," said Bolivia, pulling her Monopoly set out of the closet.

So for the next hour and a half, Rory tried his best to drive Bolivia off the game board. And by playing hard, he tried to forget for a while that he wasn't having such a great time in Ithaca.

After supper that evening, Mr. Raab drove Bolivia, Rory, and Derek to the auditorium where the ballet was being held. He was going to pick them up when it was over.

He's probably very happy he got out of this, Rory thought as he took his seat between Derek and Bolivia. He was glad none of his classmates back home could see him now. He and Derek would be laughed out of Woodside. As he looked around, Rory noticed that there were quite a few men in the audience.

"Hi, Bolivia!" a voice called out.

Rory turned to see a boy no older than six standing in the aisle near their seats.

"Alexander Gian Carlo," Bolivia called out. "These are my friends, Rory and Derek."

"My whole name is Alexander Gian Carlo Francesco Cammarata," the boy greeted Rory and Derek. "But you can call me Alexander Gian Carlo for short."

"His father teaches here at Cornell, like my parents," Bolivia explained. "And he lives next door."

"Do you like ballet?" Rory asked him. He could hardly believe that a little kid like this wanted to sit through a long and boring dance program.

"Sure," said Alexander Gian Carlo. "I take ballet lessons."

"You do?" Rory asked.

"Yes. Ballet, karate, and violin. I'm very busy."

Rory wanted to ask more, but the lights began to dim.

"Gotta get back to my seat," said Alexander Gian Carlo, and he rushed off.

"What a funny kid," Rory said.

"He's really amazingly smart for his age," said Bolivia. "He probably knows more than you do."

"Impossible," whispered Rory.

The music began and the curtains opened. Rory was embarrassed watching the male dancers, who wore skin-tight outfits that clung to their bodies. He distracted himself with thoughts of the next day. He may have given in and attended the ballet, but there was no way he was going up in the plane with Bolivia's uncle. Gradually, despite himself, Rory found his eyes were drawn to the stage. The dancers were truly amazing. Not only did the men have incredible strength, but the leaps and spins they did across the stage reminded Rory of the Olympic gymnasts he had seen on television. He wondered how many years Alexander Gian Carlo would have to study before he could do those things.

"So how did you like it?" Bolivia asked when the program ended and the curtain had fallen.

Rory stopped clapping and shrugged his shoulders. "It was okay," he said. He wasn't going to admit any more than that.

"Good," said Bolivia. She knew the answer to her question.

7
Playing Sick

On the way home from the ballet, Mr. Raab
stopped at a neighborhood ice-cream parlor.
The place was filled with college students eating
huge sundaes. Rory, Derek, and Bolivia decided to
share a concoction called the Atom Split. It com-
bined several flavors of ice cream and types of
sauce, plus bananas, fresh strawberries, nuts, and
whipped cream. As they attacked the sundae, Rory
found himself thinking once again about what lay
ahead the next day. If only this was tomorrow
night. His thoughts ruined his appetite, and he put
his spoon down. "I've had enough," he said.

"Are you sick?" asked Derek.

"Maybe I am coming down with something,"

said Rory. He might as well get them used to the idea.

"I hope not," said Bolivia. "You don't want to miss the flight tomorrow."

Back at the house again, Rory couldn't sleep. All he could do was lie in bed and think about the airplane ride. Like he had the night before, Derek fell asleep quickly, leaving Rory to toss and turn on his own. If only Derek was still awake, Rory thought he might confide in him. He wanted to talk to someone.

Rory got out of bed. The house was quiet. Bolivia's parents had gone to bed too. Only a small light was still on in the hallway.

Rory tiptoed down the hall and to the dark sun porch. He flipped the switch to turn on the light, wondering if Lucette would think it was already morning.

The parrot stirred on her perch.

"Are you sleeping?" Rory asked the bird.

"Not today. Come again," Lucette squawked at him.

"You don't get to fly much anymore," Rory said to the parrot. "Do you miss flying?"

There was no response from the parrot.

"I don't want to fly, myself," Rory whispered to the bird. "I like to keep my feet on the ground."

"Roryderek," squawked Lucette.

"That's me," said Rory. "At least, that's partly me." He reached out to touch the feathers on Lucette's head.

"I'm sorry that I woke you up," he said. "But I wanted to talk to someone." He flipped the light switch off. "Good night," he said, and he made his way back to his side of the sofa bed.

The next thing Rory knew, Derek was poking him in the ribs.

"It's time to wake up," he said. "I got up before the alarm and turned it off."

Rory sat up in bed. Sure enough, sunlight was coming in through the window.

"The weather looks perfect," said Derek. He was already half dressed.

"Yeah," said Rory.

"Well, come on. Get moving."

"I don't feel too well," said Rory very softly, as if the effort of speaking was too much for him.

"What's wrong?" asked Derek.

"I don't know. I think I'm getting a sore throat

or something. I don't think I should go out today."

"You can't be sick today," protested Derek. "We may never get another chance like this."

"I know," said Rory, trying to sound very sick and sorry at the same time. He slid back under the covers. "You and Bolivia go without me. I'll stay here."

"Gosh, you do sound awful," said Derek. "You should see a doctor."

"I'm sure it's nothing," said Rory. He might be able to fool his friends, but he didn't think he could convince a doctor that he was sick.

"I'll go get Mrs. Raab," said Derek. He rushed out of the room, leaving Rory by himself.

A moment later Bolivia's parents and Bolivia herself had come to check on Rory.

"This is awful," said Bolivia. "Rory, getting sick is not in my plans at all."

Mrs. Raab put her hand on Rory's forehead. "I don't think you have a fever," she said. "But I'll get a thermometer and find out for sure."

Bolivia's father looked so concerned that Rory felt guilty. Why couldn't they just leave?

"It's only a headache," said Rory.

"I thought you said your throat hurt," said Bolivia.

"My throat hurts *and* my head aches," said Rory. "But I'm sure I'll be better by tomorrow. I'll probably be better by this afternoon even."

"Maybe we could postpone our flight until this afternoon," said Bolivia. "I could ask Uncle Harold."

"I think I should rest all day," said Rory. He realized he had spoken in his normal voice, and whispered, hoarsely, "A good long rest will make me feel much better."

Mrs. Raab entered the bedroom, holding a thermometer in her hand. "Put this under your tongue," she said.

"If he doesn't have a temperature, could he still go up in the airplane?" asked Bolivia.

"I don't want to go up today," said Rory, but with the thermometer under his tongue, it sounded like something quite different.

"Are you sure we couldn't go tomorrow?" asked Derek.

"O ooday. O ooday," Rory insisted.

"Shhh, Rory, don't try to talk when you have the thermometer in your mouth," said Mrs. Raab. She

69

smoothed Rory's hair back and looked at him closely. "Your eyes do look a little bloodshot."

"Did you look at his tongue?" asked Bolivia.

Rory opened his mouth to show his tongue, and the thermometer slipped out onto the blanket. Mrs. Raab picked it up and held it to the light to read the numbers.

"Ninety-eight point six," she said. "That's normal."

"Then you can't be sick!" said Bolivia. "That proves it."

"Just because I don't have a temperature doesn't mean I don't feel sick," said Rory with an angry look at Bolivia.

"Of course you can feel sick without a temperature," Mrs. Raab said. "I just needed to know if you had a fever before I phoned the doctor. I think you had better spend the day right here in bed."

"It looks like Rory is in no shape to go flying," said Mr. Raab. "It's up to you two if you want to go without him."

"I can always go another time," said Bolivia. "But this is Derek's one chance. I don't think he should have to miss it just because Rory's sick."

"Rory is a guest too," Mrs. Raab reminded her daughter.

"But if Rory's coming down with something, maybe Derek and I should stay away from him, or we'll get sick too."

"That's right," put in Rory.

"Considering that you three spent all day yesterday together, you're already exposed to whatever Rory has."

"In that case, the least we can do is give Derek a good time today before he gets sick too," said Bolivia.

"My daughter, the lawyer," said Mr. Raab, smiling. "How about it, Rory? Do you mind staying here on your own while Bolivia and Derek go up with Harold in the plane?"

"It's fine with me," said Rory, trying to smile bravely.

"I have an appointment this morning," said Mrs. Raab, "but I'll leave our neighbor's phone number. Mrs. Cammarata can come over if you need her."

"I'll be fine," said Rory. "I'll probably just sleep. I won't even know you're gone."

71

"All right then, it's settled," said Mrs. Raab. "When I come back this afternoon, we'll see how you're feeling. Maybe some rest is all you need. But if you're not feeling better, we'll drive you over to Dr. Schein's office."

After everyone left the room, Rory lay back in bed and smiled. Everything had worked out for the best. Bolivia and Derek would have their flight. No one would know that he was scared. And this afternoon he'd have a miraculous recovery, and then he could enjoy the rest of his vacation.

He could hear the clatter of dishes and the chatter of voices from the dining room. He smelled bacon and eggs cooking. He hoped someone would remember to bring some breakfast to him in bed. He was wide awake now.

Mrs. Raab came into the room, carrying a glass of orange juice.

"You won't want anything to eat if you're not feeling well," she said. "But you should drink plenty of liquids."

"Thanks," said Rory. He took the juice and drained the glass. It made him feel hungrier than ever.

"Let me fix these covers for you," said Mrs.

Raab. She smoothed out the blankets and puffed up Rory's pillow. "We'll all be leaving soon. Get a good sleep and we'll see you later."

"Thanks," said Rory. This time he remembered to speak in the way he thought a sick person might.

Mrs. Raab closed the blinds to darken the room. "I've turned on our answering machine so you don't have to get out of bed," said Mrs. Raab.

"Okay," said Rory. He lay back in the bed and closed his eyes. He'd pretend to sleep until everyone left the house. Then the first thing he'd do would be to find something to eat. He might not be sick, but he was certainly dying of hunger.

8
Rory the Hero

R ory kept his eyes shut as Derek tiptoed into the room. He could tell from the noises that Derek was giving Hamlet his food.

Next Mrs. Raab came into the room for a final check. Rory lay as still as he could under the covers and hoped he convinced her that he was sleeping. He lay still for so long that he even fooled himself. The next thing he knew, he could hear the telephone ringing in the hallway. He considered jumping out of bed and taking the call for the Raabs, but then he remembered that Mrs. Raab had told him not to worry about answering the phone. The ringing stopped, and all was quiet in the house. In the half dark Rory squinted to see the time on Derek's clock. It was almost eleven thirty already.

After all that extra sleep, Rory still felt groggy. And when he swallowed, his throat did feel scratchy. His head ached too. It was crazy. Just because he'd made up a story about feeling ill, he didn't actually have to feel that way.

Rory felt a little dizzy when he got out of bed. Probably weak with hunger, he decided. It was hours and hours since he had eaten dinner last night.

On his way to the kitchen, Rory stopped at the sun porch. Lucette was preening herself on her perch. "Well," Rory announced, "I didn't want to go flying, and I didn't." His voice sounded a bit hoarse.

"Time to sleep," squawked the parrot.

"I just woke up," said Rory. "I'm going to have breakfast. You've been fed. Now it's my turn."

"Not today. Come again."

"You don't know what you're talking about," Rory said.

"Roryderek. Roryderek."

"Derek's gone flying, and I'm going to have breakfast," said Rory. Pretending to be sick was fun. But actually having a scratchy throat was putting him in a bad mood. He left Lucette and went into the kitchen.

The aroma of bacon and eggs lingered faintly in the air as Rory entered the kitchen and turned on the light. But there was another smell too, and it was a very unpleasant one. Rory looked around and noticed that Mrs. Raab had left an electric crockery pot sitting on top of the counter. Maybe the smell was coming from the pot. He wondered what Bolivia's mother was cooking. Hungry as he was, Rory certainly wouldn't want to eat whatever was making a smell like that. At least when it was served tonight, he could say he had no appetite because he was still feeling sick.

Rory opened the refrigerator and took out a container of orange juice. He found the cinnamon bread he had bought the day before. Mrs. Raab had sliced about half of the loaf, and Rory helped himself to one of the pieces. He put his slice into the toaster, but even the cinnamon smell of the toasting bread did not mask the awful odor coming from the crockery pot. What could make a fishy smell like that? Frog soup? Eel stew?

Rory could hardly eat his piece of toast. The smell in the kitchen was making him feel sick. As he stood to rinse the glass from his orange juice, he noticed that the kitchen light was flickering again.

Then there was a crackling sound and the light went out. Rory sniffed the air and realized that the odor wasn't coming from the pot after all. The smell was coming from the light fixture. It was as if something plastic or rubber was burning. Was it his imagination, or did he now see a small trickle of smoke coming from the fixture?

For a moment Rory stood undecided. It wasn't really a fire, just a little smoke. If he called the fire department, would they think he was just a silly kid? As he stood in the kitchen, trying to make up his mind, a loud, insistent beeping began. It was the smoke alarm. The sound rallied Rory. Now if he called the fire department, he could report that the fire alarm had gone off. In fact, it was making so much noise, they'd hear it for themselves.

Rory rushed to the kitchen phone and picked up the receiver. Right above the phone were the numbers for the police department and fire station. He quickly pushed the numbers.

A woman's voice answered. "Fire department," she said.

"Come quickly," said Rory. "There's a fire. At least, there's smoke and it smells awful. Can you hear the alarm? It just started going."

"Where are you?" asked the woman.

"In the kitchen. I think some wires are burning, or rubber. Something with a terrible smell."

"What's the address?" the woman asked.

"Address?"

"Yes. Where is the fire?"

"Oh," said Rory. "Let me think." He was still confused about Bolivia's address. Was it six eight six or eight six eight? Rats! He couldn't remember.

"Don't you know where you are?" asked the voice on the phone.

"I'm visiting my friend. And I forgot the address. Nobody's here but me."

"Stay calm," said the woman. "Tell me the phone number. We can trace it from here. And then leave the house at once."

Rory looked at the phone. There was no number on it. "Wait a minute," he said. "I have to look it up in the phone book."

Luckily the Ithaca phone book was right next to the telephone. Rory turned the pages as quickly as he could. "Here it is," he called into the telephone. And he recited the address.

"We'll be right there," said the woman. "Now get out of the house fast."

Rory didn't hang up the phone. He dropped it and started running toward the front door. The smoke was thicker now, but he still couldn't see any fire. As he ran, he suddenly remembered he was not alone in the house. There was Lucette, sitting on her perch in the next room. He rushed to the sun porch and grabbed the bird.

"Not today. Come again," the parrot squawked.

"Yes today. Right now," Rory shouted as he tucked the bird under his arm and rushed out the front door.

It was not until he was outside and felt the cold, damp ground under his feet that Rory realized he was not wearing any shoes. In fact, he was standing outside in his pajamas. A cool breeze ruffled Lucette's feathers and blew right through his cotton pajamas.

"Not today. Come again," Lucette squawked. "Roryderek. Roryderek."

Shivering, Rory tried to put the bird under his pajama top to keep her warm as he stood listening for the fire trucks to arrive. He heard the sound of someone rapping on a window. It was one of the Raabs' neighbors, trying to get Rory's attention from the house next door. Rory ran toward the

79

house. He had to get Lucette inside, where it was safe and warm.

"I'm Mrs. Cammarata," said the woman as soon as she opened her door. "You're one of Bolivia's friends. I saw you last night at the ballet. Why are you standing outside in your pajamas?" she asked as Rory pushed past her and into her house.

"There's a lot of smoke in the kitchen," said Rory. "The fire trucks will be here any minute," he gasped.

As he spoke, they could hear a siren approaching the house. "There they are. Can I leave Lucette here? It's too cold for her outside."

"Of course Lucette can stay here. But it's too cold for you, too."

Mrs. Cammarata opened a closet door and pulled out a coat, which she handed to Rory. "Put this on or you'll get pneumonia."

Rory took Lucette out from under his pajama top and placed her on a chair. Then he quickly put Mrs. Cammarata's coat on. It was a lady's coat, and it smelled of moth balls. The coat covered his ankles. It was a good thing Mrs. Cammarata hadn't noticed he wasn't wearing shoes. Rory rushed outside to meet the fire trucks.

Four men jumped off the first truck as it pulled up to the curb outside the Raab house. "Are you the one who called?" asked one of the men.

"Yes. The light fixture in the kitchen is burning."

Axe and hoses in hand, the fire fighters entered the house.

Suddenly Rory rushed into the house after them. "I forgot all about Hamlet," he shouted.

One of the firemen grabbed Rory by the coat. "Listen, kid, you can't come running in here. It may be dangerous."

Rory stood outside as more men rushed into the house. But in a couple of minutes, they began coming out.

"An electrical connection was burning," said one of the men. "It's a good thing you called, kid. Another ten minutes and the whole kitchen would have been in flames."

"Then Hamlet is okay?" asked Rory.

"Hamlet is dead," said the fire fighter. "I saw the movie."

"Who's dead?" asked a terrified Mrs. Cammarata. She had come out to see what was going on.

"This kid better put on some shoes, or he's not going to be too healthy," said the fireman. "But otherwise there's just a little smoke damage and a busted kitchen light."

Rory looked down at his feet, which were sticking out from Mrs. Cammarata's coat. They were freezing. "Can I go inside now?" he asked.

The fire fighter gave Rory permission to go back inside the Raab house. There was a strong smell of smoke, and cool air was coming in from windows the firemen had opened. Rory started toward the kitchen, but as he passed the living room, the sofa looked so inviting, he sat down. He pulled his feet under him and huddled inside Mrs. Cammarata's old coat. He still felt cold, even now that he was inside the house.

Mrs. Cammarata had come into the house with Rory. "You don't look very good," she said to Rory. "How do you feel?"

"I don't feel so good," Rory admitted. He lay back on the sofa, too tired to ask where Alexander Gian Carlo was this morning.

Mrs. Cammarata got a blanket for Rory. "Where's Mrs. Raab?" she asked.

"She had an appointment," said Rory, enjoying

the warmth of the blanket. "She'll be back soon."
He closed his eyes. It felt so good to close them. He
had forgotten about his headache during all the
excitement, but it felt much worse now. His throat
hurt too. Now he just wanted to rest for a little
while. . . .

Rory was sound asleep on the sofa when Mrs.
Raab came home half an hour later. And he was
still sound asleep when Mrs. Cammarata returned
home half an hour later, after explaining the events
of the morning. After Mrs. Cammarata left, Mrs.
Raab played her answering machine to see if there
were any phone messages.

Rory was just beginning to wake up when Mrs.
Raab came back into the living room to give him
the news she had found on her phone machine.

9
Unexpected News

"Rory!" Mrs. Raab exclaimed. "You are a real hero. If it wasn't for you, this whole house might have burned down. And you not only called the fire department, you rescued Lucette, too. You deserve a gold medal."

"All I did was make a phone call," said Rory. "That's not so brave." He was surprised that his voice sounded like he had a sore throat. And it hurt when he swallowed, too.

"Well, unfortunately, I don't have a gold medal to give you, just some unexpected news. It's no wonder you didn't feel up to going flying this morning," said Mrs. Raab as Rory sat up on the sofa. He was still wearing Mrs. Cammarata's coat.

Mrs. Raab put a cool hand against Rory's forehead. "You may not have had a fever this morning, but you certainly have one now."

"I don't feel so bad," said Rory.

"Well, the worst is yet to come," said Mrs. Raab. "In the midst of everything that was going on here this morning, your mother phoned and left a message. She said your sister Edna has come down with chicken pox. The doctor told her there's a very good chance that you'll get them within a few days too."

"Chicken pox?" Rory couldn't believe his ears. This morning he had only been pretending that he was sick, and now it turned out that he really was.

"Yes. You wouldn't happen to know if Derek ever had them, would you?"

"I don't think so," said Rory. "I've known him since we were both three years old. Maybe he had chicken pox before that."

"Probably not," said Mrs. Raab. "Bolivia's never had them either. I think we are in for a whole lot of chicken pox around here."

"Gosh, I'm sorry," said Rory.

"Don't apologize. You couldn't help it. And neither could your sister. Chicken pox is part of life," said Mrs. Raab. "I just feel bad that your holiday is not going to be as pleasant as planned. Bolivia wanted every moment of your visit to be just perfect."

"Chicken pox isn't a very nice bread-and-butter gift," admitted Rory. "Did you ever have chicken pox, Mrs. Raab?" It would be awful if he gave them to Bolivia's parents, too.

"Oh, yes. About a hundred years ago," laughed Mrs. Raab. "Don't worry about me. And I'm fairly certain that my husband had them when he was a kid too. If you have chicken pox once, it's very rare to get them a second time. Come on upstairs. That coat you're wearing can't be very comfortable. You must be starving, too. A little hot soup will be good for your throat. Bolivia and Derek should be back before long. They sure missed a lot while they were up in the air."

Rory started laughing along with Mrs. Raab. But his laughter turned into coughing. It was true. His friends had missed a great deal.

A little while later, Rory was propped up in Bolivia's bed with extra pillows and a tray of food in front of him. Mrs. Raab said Rory would be more comfortable there. Bolivia would sleep on the living-room sofa.

"Everything okay?" asked Mrs. Raab.

"Yes," said Rory. "How's the kitchen?"

"There's nothing the matter that an electrician can't fix. And a fresh coat of paint. I should have had that silly light fixed months ago. It never occurred to me that the flickering was a sign of a bigger problem."

"Hi. We're home." A door banged shut and a voice called out. It was Bolivia and Derek, back from flying with Uncle Harold. "What's that funny smell in the house?" asked Bolivia.

"How's Rory? Why is he in here?" asked Derek as he and Bolivia stood looking in the bedroom.

"I'm okay," Rory said. "But I've probably got chicken pox."

"Chicken pox?" said Derek and Bolivia at the same time.

"And you two are almost certainly going to get them too," said Bolivia's mother.

"You're kidding," said Bolivia.

"I wish I was. But chicken pox is very contagious, and the three of you have been together for two days."

"I'm sorry," said Rory. "But I didn't do it on purpose."

89

He scraped up the last spoonful of soup from his bowl, and Mrs. Raab took the tray from him. "There's no point in trying to separate you now, so you kids can trade stories about your day," she said.

"Oh, Rory, I wish you could have been there with us," said Bolivia.

"It was fantastic," said Derek. "I think I'll be a pilot when I grow up."

"Well, I had an adventure here, too," said Rory. "I didn't just stay in bed the whole time you were gone." He then amazed his friends with the story of the kitchen fire.

"Wow," said Derek. "Weren't you scared?"

"Well, I was afraid the fire department would think I was just a dumb kid. But once I heard the smoke alarm, I knew what I had to do."

"You were so brave to rescue Lucette. I would have just run out of the house," said Bolivia.

"Well, I did forget about Hamlet," Rory admitted. "But don't worry, Derek, he's fine. The smoke didn't get to this part of the house."

"You're still the bravest person I know," Bolivia said to Rory.

He smiled. It was funny how things had turned

out. Because he was afraid to go flying, he had stayed home and become a hero. In fact, Rory felt brave enough to admit to Bolivia and Derek that he hadn't really felt sick that morning.

"But if you weren't sick, why didn't you come with us?" asked Derek.

"I was afraid to go up in the airplane."

"You were?" said Bolivia. "Why didn't you tell us?"

"I was afraid Derek would laugh at me. And you'd think I was just making it all up to ruin your plans. You wouldn't believe I was afraid. Neither of you is afraid of anything."

"That's not true," said Bolivia. "Everyone is afraid of something. My mother is terrified of snakes."

"I was scared of something," said Derek. "I was scared of coming here."

"You were?" asked Bolivia. "What were you scared of?"

"Lots of things. I was scared your parents wouldn't like me. I was scared your mother was only going to cook weird things I didn't like. I was scared I wouldn't have a good time. But you know what? I was wrong about everything."

"You weren't wrong about the curry," Rory pointed out. Derek turned to Bolivia. "I bet you're never scared of anything."

"I was scared of inviting you guys to come and visit."

"Really?" said Rory.

"I was afraid that you wouldn't like it here," said Bolivia. "I was afraid that something awful would happen. I almost didn't invite you. And when I did, I planned every single second of the visit, so it would go just perfectly."

"Well, it hasn't gone perfectly," said Rory. "Not with me getting chicken pox."

"But I'm glad we came," said Derek.

"I'm glad you both came," said Bolivia.

"No one else except you knows that I'm afraid of airplanes," said Rory. "My parents don't even know. Promise me you won't tell."

"Shake," said Derek holding out his hand. "And promise that you won't tell I was scared of coming here."

"Shake," said Bolivia.

Mrs. Raab came into the room as the three friends were making their three-handed shake. "I've got more news for you," she said.

"What is it?" asked Bolivia.

"Rory and Derek will have to extend their visit," said Mrs. Raab. "They can't go traveling home on the bus, giving chicken pox to everyone they meet."

"Wow!" said Derek.

"No kidding?" said Rory.

"Well, the longer they can stay here, the better I like it," said Bolivia. "Chicken pox and all."

10
Stuck in the House

There was always the chance that Derek or Bolivia might not catch chicken pox. Still, it didn't seem right for them to go off and leave Rory alone. And if they were coming down with chicken pox, it wouldn't be good to expose other people to it as well. "Just think of all those college students on the bus coming here," said Derek.

"Maybe they had chicken pox when they were younger," said Rory, imagining an entire college closed down because of a chicken-pox epidemic caused by him.

So Derek and Bolivia mostly stayed home.

"If only you had a TV," sighed Rory, trying hard not to scratch his itchy pox.

"We don't need a TV," said Bolivia. "I'll think up plenty of things for us to do."

If anyone could come up with new ideas, it was Bolivia. Sure enough, she was soon explaining a new game she had made up. For a whole afternoon they pretended they were shipwrecked on a desert island, eating only the chocolate-chip cookies they'd salvaged when their ship went down. Derek used Bolivia's binoculars, and they all avoided the living-room rug, which was a river filled with man-eating crocodiles.

They played more traditional games as well, like Monopoly, backgammon, and Chinese checkers. And they even started to write a spooky ghost story together.

In fact, they managed to entertain themselves so well that when Mr. Raab arrived home one day, carrying a borrowed TV set, they hardly noticed. They were too busy to sit around and watch television.

Then Uncle Harold came for a visit. Unlike Alexander Gian Carlo, who could only shout to them from his window, Uncle Harold came inside. He had had chicken pox when he was a kid.

"I hear that Rory saved the day," he said. He

seemed about to slap Rory on the back but then thought better of it. "And I've also heard that you guys are sticking around town a bit longer," he added.

"We can't go home like this," said Rory, pointing to his face, which was covered with chicken pox scabs. "Derek has them now too."

"I have a plan for when you are both feeling better," said Uncle Harold. "I have to go to New York City on some business next week. How would you like to fly down with me? Of course, I'd have to clear it with your parents."

Taking a quick look at Rory, Bolivia said, "They can't go with you, Uncle Harold. They have round-trip bus tickets."

"That's no problem," said Uncle Harold. "They can get a refund."

"Thank you," said Derek. "But I think I'd prefer to take the bus home."

"Why, Derek? Didn't you enjoy flying with me the other day?"

"Oh, yes," said Derek, the parts of his face that weren't covered with chicken pox turning red as he tried to think of some excuse.

"It's all right, Derek," said Rory, surprised to

hear his own words. "I think I'd like to fly home. Don't forget, I didn't have a chance to go up with Bolivia's uncle, like you did." For some reason, even though he still felt a twinge of fear, Rory sensed that he was ready. He liked being Rory the hero. And what was the point of being a hero if he was afraid to go up in an airplane?

"But, Rory, we had so much fun on the bus," said Derek.

"Why don't you fellows think about it?" suggested Uncle Harold. "I'm not going until next week. You can let me know what you decide."

"That's a good idea," said Bolivia.

Uncle Harold stayed for supper, and it was not until after he left that Bolivia, Rory, and Derek could talk about his offer.

"I know how you feel about flying, Rory," said Derek.

"And I know how much you want to fly again," said Rory.

"I had a chance to fly," said Derek. "I don't have to go again so soon."

"No," said Rory. "I've been thinking about this all evening, and I'm ready to do it. Honest."

"Good," said Bolivia. Her head had been turning back and forth from one boy to the other.

"I refuse," said Derek. "You can't make me. I want to take the bus."

"Wait a minute. This is getting confusing," said Bolivia. "Derek doesn't want to fly because Rory hates flying, but Rory wants to fly because Derek loves it, even though he is now saying he doesn't? It's like watching a tennis game."

"Listen, you guys," said Rory. "Everyone said I was brave because of what happened during the fire. But you know what? I wasn't brave at all. I just did it. Brave is when you are afraid of something and you do it anyway. That's why I want to fly. Honest. Cross my heart and hope to die." Then, realizing what he said, Rory added, "I just hope we don't die in the airplane."

11
Up, Up, and Away

So that was why on Thursday, April 23, a week later than planned, and on transportation neither boy could originally have dreamed of, Rory Dunn and Derek Curry and a hamster named Hamlet flew home to Woodside, New Jersey, from Ithaca, New York, with Bolivia's uncle Harold.

Rory looked a bit pale as they boarded the plane. Everyone thought it was the aftermath of his bout of chicken pox. Derek, who was recovering from the same ailment, didn't look pale at all. But that's how it is. People don't always react the same way to the same things.

Because it was his first flight, Rory was seated by Uncle Harold in the front, next to the pilot's seat.

Derek sat right behind him, with his camera ready to take pictures.

Rory pulled the strap of his seatbelt extra tight. It wouldn't be of much use in an accident. Still, the belt made him feel slightly more secure. Helped by Bolivia and Derek, he had not eaten any breakfast that morning. Bolivia had drunk his orange juice and eaten his slice of toast and Derek had gobbled up his scrambled eggs while Mrs. Raab's back was turned. Rory knew that if his stomach was empty, he would not throw up on Uncle Harold, no matter what else happened on board the plane.

Uncle Harold turned some knobs and pushed some buttons, and the plane's propeller began to spin, making an enormous noise. Soon the propeller was going so fast that you couldn't make it out at all. Then the plane began to taxi down the runway like a speeding car. That part was fun. But a moment later Rory knew they were no longer on the ground.

"If you look to the right," said Uncle Harold, "you'll see the highway underneath us. It runs right into State Street, where you were staying."

"Too bad we can't wave to Bolivia," Derek called from the backseat.

Bolivia was home from school with a fever and what certainly looked like the beginnings of chicken pox.

Rory's hands gripped the bottom of his seat as he looked down. He saw a bright spot of blue below and pointed to it. "Is that a river?" he asked.

"It's Cayuga Lake. Next time you come up here, I'll take you out on it in my canoe," said Uncle Harold.

"If we survive," Rory said to himself. He could still hardly believe that he had been able to get on the airplane. At this very minute he could have been sitting on a bus with its wheels all safely rolling along the ground.

The plane flew higher, and Uncle Harold continued to point out landmarks that he recognized along the way. Rory couldn't always hear what Bolivia's uncle was saying. The plane made a lot of noise.

Rory studied the dials and knobs in front of him. He hoped there was enough fuel. You couldn't stop at a gas station in mid-air. They flew through a cloud, and then they were in clear sky with the sun shining down. Rory saw a dark spot on the ground below. It was the shadow of their plane, following them as they flew along.

He could see fields and farms. There were faint green lines across the fields, perhaps corn just beginning to grow.

Rory's stomach rumbled. He was actually feeling hungry. His hands loosened on the seat, and he turned around to smile at Derek. Derek was holding his camera. Hamlet's box was at his feet.

"Guess what?" Rory said.

"What?" asked Derek.

"This is fun. I like it."

Derek picked up his camera and aimed at his friend through the viewfinder. "I knew you would," he said as he pushed the shutter button. "I'm glad."

"I'm glad too," said Rory. He was wearing the red fez from Turkey. Bolivia had given it to him just before he left.

"Hey. You can't give me this," Rory had said.

"Sure I can," said Bolivia. "It's your reward for being so brave." And she did.

And he was.

* * *

Dear Bolivia,

I have a *ton* of homework. You can't believe how much work Derek and I missed in just one week.

But I wanted to tell you what a great time I had, even though most of the time I had the chicken pox. Still, it was much more fun having chicken pox at your house than it would have been at home.

Are you coming back here for the summer? I'll let you wear the fez if you do.

Your friend,

Rory the Hero

About the Author

JOHANNA HURWITZ is the award-winning author of many popular books for young readers, including *The Adventures of Ali Baba Bernstein, Aldo Applesauce, Rip-Roaring Russell, Class Clown,* and *Baseball Fever.* She has worked as a children's librarian in school and public libraries in New York City and Long Island. She frequently visits schools around the country to talk about books with students, teachers, librarians, and parents.

Mrs. Hurwitz and her husband live in Great Neck, New York, and are the parents of two grown children.